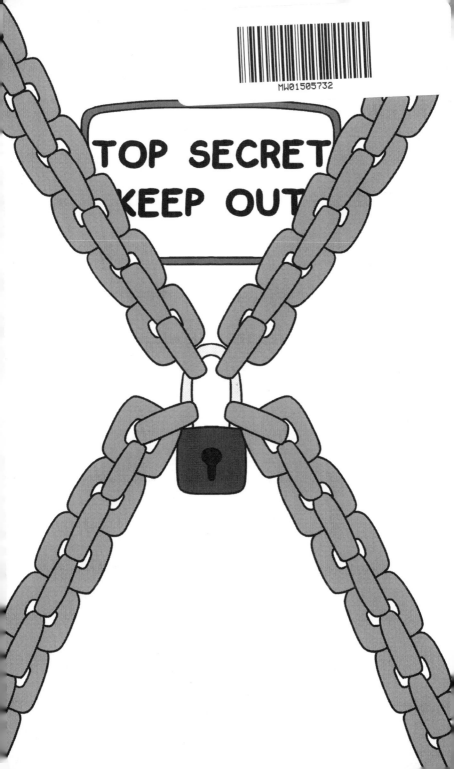

Mac's Mission Diary:
Operation Save the Summer

By S.J. Engelman

ISBN 978-1-7345670-4-5

Characters and events in this book are fictitious. Any similarity to real persons, living or dead, is coincidental and not intended by the author.

Illustrations by Afif Amrullah

Published by Inkwell Media, LLC
Indianapolis, Indiana

Visit www.StephanieEngelman.com

For Zach, Morgan, Isaac,
Mary Lise, and Evan

Best. Family. Ever.
(Because you're in it.)

MISSING

Jerry

Trusted friend and source of
endless entertainment

Height: 10 inches

Color: Black

Last seen June 1 at 9:34 pm

Monday, June 2, 8:30 a.m.

Dear Mission Diary,

My name is Mac McMillan, and I am a kid on a mission.

My most treasured possession in the whole world is gone, stolen by a thief in the night.

I last saw Jerry right before I went to bed last night. I was careful to set the controller right beside him so he'd be all set to play when I got up this morning. An evil

1

villain had other plans, however.

When I woke up today, I stayed in bed for a long time because — guess what? — I could. No alarm, no rushing off to school, no sitting at a desk all day. I put my hands behind my head, stared at the ceiling, and thought about all the great things I have planned for summer vacation.

When I finally got out of bed, I made a bee line toward Jerry — or, at least, toward where Jerry should have been. Instead, I found nothing but a few dust bunnies and some disconnected cords under the TV.

The most likely suspect was my older brother, Luke, who's been known to take Jerry to a friend's house and leave him there for days. I went straight back to our room, climbed up to Luke's bed, and began my interrogation.

"I didn't take Jerry, you idiot!" Luke grabbed the pillow from my hands, rolled over, and covered his head with the pillow.

Assuming he was telling the truth, that left only one suspect:

MOM!!

I raced downstairs, yelling her name the whole way down.

I found her in the kitchen.

"Yes, dear?" she said, her lips curled in a fake smile.

"Did you take Jerry?!!!"

"I don't know any 'Jerry,'" she said, "but if you're talking about the video game console, the answer is, 'Yes. I did.'"

"Why???!!!"

"Because good moms don't let their sons waste their summers playing video games." Her smile grew even more fake. "And I generally like to think I'm a good mom."

"Good moms don't take away their sons' only form of entertainment and leave them with nothing to do all summer!" I challenged.

"You're right. That's why I didn't take away the trampoline, or your bike, or your scooter, or the basketball hoop, or the ping-pong table, or ... Well, you get the point."

"Mom. You totally don't get it. None of

those things are fun without my friends, and I can't talk to my friends without Jerry."

Mom rolled her eyes. "Seriously, Mac. That little black box is not your pet. Stop calling it Jerry."

I wanted to roll my eyes right back at her, but I knew that would just get me in trouble. Instead, I talked really slow. "Mom. I've explained a bazillion times: Little kids name their teddy bears. Big kids name their cars. In-between kids name their gaming consoles, and my console is named Jerry."

"Well, whatever you want to call it, it's just a machine, and — yes — I took it. As I said, you have lots of other things you can do this summer."

"Mom, he's how I talk to my friends. I need him so we can make plans."

"We have a phone, Mac, and you can use it anytime you want." She waved a hand around like this would solve everything. "Regardless, you can have your precious 'Jerry' once you've finished your summer reading and written 50 pages in your journal."

"WHAT journal?"

"This journal," she said. "It arrived in the mail yesterday." And she held up this awful, empty book in which I am currently writing.

"50 pages?!!" I yelled. "Mom, I can never write 50 pages!"

"Oh, yes, you can," she sang in a high-pitched voice. "You can write about all the fun things you do this summer, what you're thankful for, your goals and things you want to do during vacation. You can even write when you're angry or frustrated about something." She handed me the book. "You never know. You might find it really helpful," she added, and she smiled like the subject was closed.

The subject WASN'T closed, though, and just to make sure Mom knew it, I threw the stupid journal on the floor.

Mom stopped in her tracks, turned around, and crossed her arms. "Mac McMillan, pick that up right now."

I crossed my arms, too, and didn't move.

"Make that 75 pages you need to write."

I stood my ground.

"100 pages."

My fingers twitched. I didn't want to do it. Everything in me screamed, "NO, MAC, DON'T PICK UP THE STUPID JOURNAL!!!!" But if there's one thing I know about Mom, it's that she was about to go to 150.

I could feel the heat rising in my face as I bent down. I grabbed the book in two fingers and held it at arms' length, like it might bite me if it were any closer.

"Wise choice," Mom said, and she took a step closer. "Mac, I love you and I want what's best for you." She wrapped an arm around my shoulder. "Like I said, you may find writing in the journal helpful." She raised her eyebrows. "You might actually like it."

I shook my head. "It's the dumbest thing ever, Mom, and I'm never going to like it."

"I'll tell you what," she said. "You can add pictures, too. That will help fill 100 pages, and getting your video games back will serve as your motivation."

With that, Mom gave me one last squeeze, turned, and walked away. I stood there fuming, and I made up my mind.

MOM DOESN'T KNOW WHAT TRUE "MOTIVATION" IS!

SHE'S TURNED ME INTO A KID ON A MISSION, AND I WILL NOT GIVE UP UNTIL I ACHIEVE MY OBJECTIVE!

I'll read the boring summer reading. I have to for school, anyways. I will write in this stupid "journal" to make her THINK I'm doing what she wants.

But I WILL NOT let my mom destroy my entire summer in the meantime!

This is not some lame journal. Its blank pages won't be used to write about my stupid feelings, goals, or any of that other dumb stuff.

No. THIS is a MISSION DIARY, with which I hereby initiate the mission:

OPERATION SAVE THE SUMMER

I WILL get Jerry back. It may not be today. It may not be tomorrow. But it will be a whole lot sooner than the FOREVER my evil mother is talking about!

Dear Mission Diary,

With nothing better to do, I've spent the day considering the challenge before me, and here's what I realized: Mom doesn't know what she's up against.

She always says video games are bad for you and that they turn your brain into mush. I've tried to convince her just how wrong she is, but she won't even listen to me. Now it's time to show her.

Video games have taught me to survive through my own creativity.

I've spawned in barren and desolate places, where I had no food, no weapons, no shelter.

I've planted farms.

I've cut down trees.

I've made my own weapons.

I've mined ore and made MORE weapons.

I've fought off zombies and ghosts.

I've run from angry mobs. I've trapped the mob. I'VE ESCAPED THE MOB!!!

Mom thinks all that was useless, just because I was doing it in a video game. It wasn't, though. All that time, I was learning, growing stronger, smarter, and BETTER.

Now, I'm about to show her just how STRONG, just how SMART, just how BETTER Mac McMillan has become.

Here's the best news: there are no angry mobs or man-eating zombies in my house. I already have shelter, and, without even knowing she's done it, Mom has provided almost all the weapons I will need.

I've created a four-pronged attack, and I KNOW at least one of these prongs will succeed! Now I can sit back, survey the landscape, and determine the best plan of attack.

THE FOUR-PRONGED APPROACH

Search for — and find! — Jerry

Go on a hunger strike

Make some $$ and buy another Jerry

Report Mom for child neglect (LAST RESORT! Only if necessary)

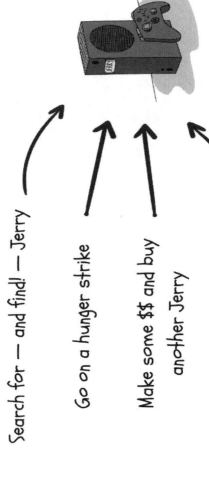

Tuesday, June 3, 8:00 a.m.

Dear Mission Diary,

Last night, I went undercover as Mac-Not-Having-Fun. I jumped on the trampoline. I shot baskets. I rode my scooter. I even tried doing all three at once.

The whole time, though, I was thinking about my mission. I considered the pros and cons of each plan of attack, took an inventory of all my resources, and spent some time observing the adversary (AKA Mom.)

After all that, here's what I figured out: My very best asset is none other than ...

(drum roll, please)

Mom.

That's right. It may sound crazy, but it's true. Last night, she was all worried about whether I ate my vegetables. The minute I complained I didn't get any strawberries, she cut up more. If I stop eating, she won't be able to stand it. She'll cave and let me have Jerry back for sure.

The battle plan is set.

I'm going on a hunger strike.

Right after I eat a few of the donuts Mom just brought home.

Tuesday, June 3, 9:45 a.m.

Dear Mission Diary,

My little sister, Elizabeth, is mad at me because I ate "her" donuts. I had to, though. Mom only got two donuts for each of us, and I figured that wasn't enough to get me through the whole day.

Now I feel like I'm about to puke, so eating's about the last thing I want to do. I figure that's a great beginning to a hunger strike.

Another good thing is, I'm actually finding this "mission diary" kind of useful. I guess it's not so bad that Mom's making me write in it. Still, there's no way I'll write 100 pages and, since she said I could add pictures, I figure I'll draw some enormous ones, like this:

(That's me puking up all those donuts.

Maybe drawing it will make it happen and then I'll start to feel better?)

Tuesday, June 3, 1:15 p.m.

Dear Mission Diary,

Well, I sat with the puke bucket for a while, but nothing came up. Finally, I laid down and fell asleep. I felt a lot better by the time Mom woke me up for lunch, which would have been a good thing, except that I was starving.

The good news is, I'm still starving, which means my hunger strike has really, truly begun.

Mom made fish sticks for lunch. I swear they looked something like this:

They smelled even worse than they looked, so not eating them was easy. I sat back and waited for Mom to notice.

Unfortunately, she had made the horrible mistake of putting tartar sauce on the plate of my four-year-old brother, Matthew, so she was too busy dealing with his fit to even notice I wasn't eating.

Finally, after everybody else had gotten up from the table, I pushed my chair back super hard so it hit the wall behind me.

"Mac!" Mom finally remembered I existed. "You need to be more careful!"

"Sorry," I said. "But I'm done, and—" I held my plate out so she could see all the food was still there. "—I'm TAKING MY PLATE TO THE SINK."

Mom was engrossed in cleaning up Matthew's tartar-sauce mess, and didn't even look at me. "Okay," she said. "Please rinse it off and put it in the dishwasher."

"What do you want me to do with all this food I didn't eat?" I asked, holding the plate closer to her face.

"You could try packing it up and sending it to the starving children of the world," she smirked, "but it probably won't taste very good by the time it reaches them."

It probably didn't taste very good from the moment it came out of the oven. But I didn't say that.

"Seriously, Mom. Should I just throw it all away?"

She put her hands on her hips. "Mac, you need to eat something. If it's not going to be fish sticks, make yourself a peanut butter and jelly sandwich or something."

"I can't." My heart started beating fast, and I felt that prickly feeling in my hands I always get when I'm nervous.

"Mac, you are perfectly capable of making a PB-n-J."

"No, I mean I couldn't EAT a peanut butter and jelly sandwich, even if I made it."

"Are you suddenly allergic to peanut butter?"

"No."

"Gluten?"

"No."

"Deathly afraid that the peanut butter

19

will glue your tongue to the roof of your mouth?"

I rolled my eyes. "No, Mom."

"Well then, why can't you eat a peanut butter and jelly sandwich? You love PB-n-J."

The prickles in my hands got stronger. "Because I'm on a hunger strike." I held my breath and waited.

Here's what I expected to happen:

Mom didn't freak out, though. Instead, she cocked her head to one side, raised an eyebrow, and said, "Huh. I'm guessing this is about the gaming console?"

I nodded.

She shrugged. "Fair enough."

I couldn't believe it. I'm going to starve myself and my own mother just shrugs, like she couldn't care less?!

Then she said, "Well, if you're going to go hungry, you might as well use it for good. Why don't you offer it up for all the people who truly ARE starving in this world?"

"Mom! I'm STARVING MYSELF because you won't let me play video games!"

"Yes, Mac. I understand that. And you don't know what true hunger is. So, every time you think about being hungry," she looked at the plate I'd forgotten I was holding, "I suggest you pray for the millions of people who are hungry but don't have plates full of food they're about to dump in the trash."

I stomped into the kitchen and made as much noise as I possibly could cleaning off my plate. Mom came in and handed me Matthew's plate.

"How's about you try again?" she said. "This time a little more quietly."

I wasn't sure it was possible, but I made even more noise the second time around.

"And again," Mom said, and she handed me the nasty pan she'd cooked the fish sticks on.

21

I made a point of tip-toeing around the kitchen. When the opportunity came to let the pan clatter into the dishwasher, though, I couldn't resist.

"The toilet in your bathroom needs to be cleaned," Mom sang.

There's nothing I hate more than cleaning toilets. Plus, scrubbing toilets on an empty stomach is probably even worse than scrubbing them on a full one. Mom handed me a whole stack of dishes, and I cleaned each of them, almost without a sound.

Still, I think I'm making progress in my mission. Mom might be all shrugs and "fair-enoughs," but for a mom that's always worried about what her kids eat, me not eating at all has got to be killing her.

Tuesday, June 3, 7:45 p.m.
(AKA the LONGEST DAY EVER)

Dear Mission Diary,

Ask me what my favorite food is. Just ask.

Okay, fine. I'll tell you.

Steak.

Guess what my family had for dinner tonight?

Yep.

Steak.

It smelled UH-MAY-ZING. Plus, there were mashed potatoes and fresh-baked rolls, not to mention strawberry shortcake with whipped cream for dessert — all of which Mom made sure I helped pass around the table.

She says she planned the meal for days, but I don't believe her. I think Mom made the world's best home-made dinner just to torture me.

It worked. My stomach growled the whole time and hasn't stopped since. Mom forced me to sit at the table until everyone was done and Dad, of course, had thirds.

I'm not very good at math, but I counted

the hours, so I know: It's been ten and a

half hours since I last ate, and I'm starving. Really, truly, seriously starving.

Luke was up in his loft bed face-timing his girlfriend, Lilly, when I hit the ten-hour mark. I climbed up his ladder and told him.

"I haven't eaten for ten hours."

He rolled his eyes. "Wow."

"So, do you think I'll have to go to the hospital if I keep this up much longer?"

"No, dude. You can go, like, forty days without eating."

"No way. I'm already lightheaded."

"Dude. Jesus went forty days in the desert without food OR water."

"Yeah, but that was Jesus."

"True."

The girlfriend could hear the whole conversation, of course, so she chimed in. "I heard Gandhi went 21 days without food, more than once."

"Look it up, bro," Luke said, "but I'm pretty sure you're not going to die anytime soon. Now, get off my ladder."

He went back to talking to Lilly, and I climbed down and got on the computer.

Sure enough, Lilly was right. Gandhi did go without food for 21 days — not once, not twice, but THREE times.

Here's me if I don't eat for 21 days:

Even worse, there are records of people surviving 40 days without food — people who WEREN'T Jesus.

Here's me after 40 days with no food:

I might need to change my mission plan.

Dear Mission Diary,

Why starve to death, when all I really need to do is make Mom THINK I'm starving to death? Therefore, I have decided to alter my mission plan slightly.

I set things in motion last night while Mom was getting Matthew ready for bed and Dad was outside talking to a neighbor. First, I went into the kitchen and ate the leftover strawberry shortcake. There wasn't any whipped cream left, but the goal is worth the sacrifice. Next, I filled the bottom of my shirt with granola bars and, just to be healthy, grabbed a banana from the counter, too.

Next, I snuck up to my room and ate three granola bars. Since someone would see the wrappers if I threw them in the trash can, I stuck them at the end of my bed under the sheets. Then I hid the rest of the granola bars in my desk drawer and hurried back downstairs to make it look like I'd been watching TV the whole time.

Mom totally fell for it. Only problem was, I was starving again when I woke up this morning.

No problem, right? After all, I still had a

bunch of granola bars and a banana stashed in my desk. I climbed down from my bed, mouth watering. When I got to the bottom of my ladder, though, I saw something terribly suspicious.

Those weren't my wrappers.

I ran to my desk and opened the drawer. There was one granola bar left. ONE!

Before I even knew what I was doing, I'd climbed Luke's ladder. He'd buried his head under the covers, so I had to settle for banging the granola bar on his blanket instead of his face.

"Bro! What're you doing?!" he poked his head out and threw his pillow at me.

"YOU ATE MY GRANOLA BARS!" I hissed as loudly as I dared.

"Dude. I was doing you a favor."

"A favor! I'm starving, and you call eating my granola bars a FAVOR?"

"Bro, you were breaking your own hunger strike. Mom would have found out, and then you'd have starved yourself all day for no reason. So, I did you a favor and ate all the granola bars, except one. I figure one won't totally kill your strike."

"I must've had twenty granola bars in there! How did you eat them all?"

"Actually there were eight granola bars, and eating seven of them was easy. The banana was a little under-ripe, but I managed to choke it down. I was hungry." He pulled the covers back over his head. "Now, get off my ladder." He stuck his hand out from under the blanket. "And hand me my pillow."

I climbed down the ladder, picked up his stupid pillow, climbed back up, and hit him over the head with it. Twice. He laughed and pushed me off the ladder.

If I could trade Luke for Jerry right now, I would.

Dear Mission Diary,

Since I had nothing better to do this morning, I decided to get started on my summer reading. The school only said I have to read 300 pages of any book, so I went into my little brother room and read every book on his bookshelf. That got me 153 pages — DONE.

But then I told Mom about my progress.

"Wow, Mac. One hundred and fifty-three pages. That's impressive! When did you become such a fast reader?"

I shrugged.

"Hmmm," Mom said. "What book are you reading?"

I was suddenly absorbed in using my toe to try to get a spot of dried-up slime out of the carpet.

"Mac?"

"Yeah?" I looked at her innocently.

"In what book did you read 153 pages?"

"Well, it wasn't just one book," I confessed. "It was, like, eight."

For a writer, Mom's surprisingly good at math. "So, you read eight books, each averaging ..." she thought for a split second "... less than 20 pages."

I shrugged and tried to deflect. "Who was it that got this slime on the carpet?"

"Your little sister, and don't change the subject. Exactly what eight books did you read?"

"Go, Dog, Go," I said, wishing the slime would open into a Mac-sized hole, "and Goodnight Moon, Where the Wild Things Are, and—" Mom started to laugh, so I threw in one I thought she'd like "—Baby's First Bible Stories!"

Mom laughed even harder. Once she'd finally calmed down, she said, "Obviously, those books are not age-appropriate. You can't count them toward your summer reading."

"But, MOM. The school didn't say my summer reading had to be 'age appropriate.'"

"You're right, Mac. They didn't. That's because it goes without saying."

"Well, I read all those books! It has to count for something!"

Mom nodded her head and thought for a second, then acted like she had some brilliant idea. "Here you go. A book at your reading level probably averages about 200 words per page. So, here's what I want you to do: Go add up all the words on all those 153 pages you read. We'll divide by 200, and you'll get credit for whatever number we come up with."

"But Mom—!"

"Ah ah!" She held up a finger. "No buts. It's that or no credit. Now, go get it done."

So I did it.

It took forever, but finally I had a number: 1752

Mom made me do the division myself — on PAPER, with a PENCIL. No calculator.

1752 divided by 200 is 8.76

Mom told me she'd count it as nine. I argued.

"I was being generous with nine pages, Mac. Since you want to argue, you can read this, as well." She grabbed the nearest book and handed it to me. "That'll get you to nine."

I looked at the book. <u>Pinkalicious</u>.

"But, Mom, that's a girl b—"

Mom started to grab another book. I shut up and started reading.

Once I'd finished <u>Pinkalicious,</u> Mom gave me some stupid book about some stupid kid that climbed a bunch of stupid mountains. The first thing I did was flip to the back of the book. 368 pages. Which is nuts. I've never read a book that long!

I counted the words on the first full page. It doesn't just have 200 words on it. It has 258 words. My mom is CRAZY if she thinks I'm going to read 368 pages with 258 words on every page!

I did some math and told her: if the average age-appropriate book has 200 words per page, and this book has 258 words per page, I should only have to read 232.5 pages of this book.

Shockingly, Mom said that was fine.

"In fact," she said, "you can read 223.5 pages, since you've already read nine pages from Matthew's books."

I'll count this as a win.

Dear Mission Diary,

My cousin Zeke called yesterday and asked if I could go swimming at the Rivi with him. This was good on two counts: the Rivi's enormous pool would give me something fun to do, plus I'd be able to get a cheeseburger and fries at the snack bar without Mom knowing about it.

When we pulled into the parking lot, however, there were two firetrucks sitting out front. Just my dumb luck, they'd had a fire in the snack bar. It was closed for the rest of the afternoon.

No cheeseburger, no fries, no nothing.

Which leads me to this fact: I'm sick and tired of granola bars. Therefore, I've decided to move forward with multiple angles of my battle plan.

I'll keep doing the fake hunger strike, meaning I won't eat in front of Mom, Dad, or anyone that will tattle-tale on me. BUT I'm going to search the house for Jerry today. I might not be able to play video games while Mom's home, but I can hook him up and play whenever she's not.

If I can't find him, I'll start saving money to buy a new Jerry. If I buy him with my own money, she won't be able to take him from me anymore!

Of course, the new one won't be Jerry. It will be Jerry's brother, Harry. Or Barry. Or . . . whatever. The name doesn't matter, so long as I have a replacement for Jerry.

Meanwhile, I still have to get the stupid summer reading and journaling done, so I'll keep working on that, too.

And I figure I'll do a little research to see what counts as child neglect, just in case nothing else works.

I'll keep you posted.

Thursday, June 5, 10:45 a.m.

Dear Mission Diary,

I just searched, "What counts as child neglect" on the computer. Here's what I found:

"Neglect is the ongoing failure to meet a child's basic needs and is the most common form of child abuse. A child may be left hungry, dirty, without adequate clothing, shelter, supervision, medical or health care. A child may be put in danger or not protected from physical or emotional harm."

I'm going to wait a couple days to see if maybe Mom will cave, but it's good to know the "child neglect" angle is an option. She's definitely leaving me hungry, and not having Jerry for company is absolutely putting me in danger of emotional harm.

Now for the bad news: While I was on the computer, I went ahead and looked up how much another gaming console would cost. The latest and greatest model was literally more money than I've made in my entire life, and last year's model wasn't much better.

I searched and I searched, and finally I

found a USED console just like Jerry for $200.
That seemed do-able.

And then I went and counted all the money
I have in my "SAVE" jar.

   $3.27

Not good. I could save up my whole
allowance all summer, and I still wouldn't
have $200. That's OK, though, because there
are other ways to make money — including
lemonade stands. Elizabeth's always wanting
to do one, so I'll get her to do it with me. If
we can make $50, I'll be a quarter of the way
there. If we did that for four days, I'd have a
new (okay, used) console!

Operation Save the Summer is going
strong.

Dear Mission Diary,

I started looking for Jerry yesterday, and I didn't find him. I did make progress on another aspect of the mission, though.

There's this kid named Grayson whose dad lives behind us. I met him once before, but he's usually at his mom's house, so we've never hung out — until yesterday, when I was jumping on the trampoline. Grayson came out into his backyard and started throwing the ball for his dog. Since he looked super bored, I asked him if he wanted to come over and jump on the trampoline with me. After we'd jumped for a while, we got to talking. I told him Elizabeth and I were going to do a lemonade stand, and he wanted to do it with us. Plus, he said he had some cookies we could sell, too.

We waited until after lunch — which I didn't eat, of course — and then we set up the lemonade and cookie stand. Business was slow, but I got to drink all the lemonade I wanted, since starving myself only applies to food. Plus, whenever Elizabeth wasn't looking, I got to eat a cookie.

By 4:30, we'd only made $8. Somehow, though, we'd gone through four pitchers of lemonade and all of Grayson's cookies.

Grayson and I didn't want to do the math to divide $8 three ways, so I said we should sell two more cups of lemonade to make it an easy $9. Pretty soon, all the neighbors started coming home from work and we ended up making three more bucks. Eleven wasn't any easier to split between the three of us, but we figured it out anyway. Grayson and Elizabeth walked away with $6.33, and, since the whole lemonade stand was my idea in the first place, they let me have the extra penny.

That means I've made $6.34 so far. At this rate, it will take 31.59 days to earn enough money to buy the used console.

On the bright side, 31.59 days is better than the 40 days it might take me to starve to death, if I were really starving myself. Which I'm not, of course.

The moral of this entry is: Lemonade stands are good, but I need another source of income.

Dear Mission Diary,

It's raining outside and I have nothing better to do than fill a few pages of this stupid journal, so I figure I'll tell you about my family. Here goes ...

The first thing you should know is that we're kind of weird. Why's that, you ask? Well, for one thing there are a lot of us. Seven, to be exact, when you include Mom and Dad.

The other thing that makes us weird is my parents. There's Mom, who's so uber-Catholic, she goes to Mass on the weekdays and wakes up in the middle of the night to go to the church and pray. She's also a writer who spends most of her working hours sitting in a coffee shop making up stories. If that's not weird, I don't know what is.

Then there's my dad. Other kids' dads mow the lawn, grill hamburgers, coach their kids' sports teams, and play golf. My dad used to do that kind of stuff, but then he started his own business. Now he mostly just works, pretty much all the time, which is a real bummer. His hamburgers used to be the best, and Luke says he's an awesome coach. I wouldn't know.

Dad's already promised to coach my basketball team next year, though, so hopefully it'll get better soon. And, man, what I wouldn't give for one of his hamburgers right about now.

Anyways ... other than that, I guess we're relatively normal. You've met my brother Luke, and you know he's a jerk, like most older brothers. Then there's my sister Clare, who likes to wear makeup and talk on the phone all the time. She's also a total drama queen and freaks out over the dumbest things — like a hair in her food or sitting on the toilet when somebody left the seat up.

I'm the middle kid in the family, and "middle" pretty much sums me up. I do okay but not great at school, I'm okay but not awesome at most sports, I'm not a cool kid but I'm not uncool, either. If you line up all the kids in my grade by height, you'll find me in — you guessed it — the middle.

One thing I'm NOT "middle" at is how I came into this world.

You see, seven weeks before I was supposed to be born, I decided I was ready to come out and meet my crazy family. Unfortunately, my body wasn't quite as ready as I was, so I had to hang out at the hospital for a long time to get everything working right. For a while, the doctors said I shouldn't even eat the normal way, so mom had to feed me through a tube.

Fortunately, I have no memory of those

days, and I've been eating the old-fashioned way ever since I can remember ... except for the last few days, of course, when I've barely been eating at all.

It was thanks to my long stay in the hospital that I wound up being called Mac instead of Michael — which I'm actually very grateful for. There isn't another "Mac" in my grade, or even in my whole school, so that's one other thing that I'm not totally "middle" about.

Here's how my name got changed:

When I was still living in a heated box at the hospital, Dad nailed the letters of my name above my crib back home. While nobody was paying attention, Luke climbed into the crib and messed with the letters. He threw a few of them on the floor and moved the "A" in between the "M" and the "C." Mom came home, saw it, and said it was meant to be.

"Our last name is McMillan, and the doctor who delivered you was Dr. MacDowell!" Mom likes to tell me. "So now you're not just named after St. Michael—" that's the angel that threw Satan out of Heaven "—you're also named after the doctor who saved your life — not to mention our family name!"

Whatever the reason, I guess it's one nice thing Luke has done for me, even if he didn't mean to.

Back to the family:

Elizabeth comes after me, and she's not

average at anything. Instead, she's super everything — super weird, super loud, super annoying, even super skinny. She likes to pretend she's a dog, a cat, or a hamster — whatever pet she happens to want that day, and she likes to pretend she's a teacher, which is super stupid, since she's not smart enough to teach anybody anything, not even a four-year-old.

The four-year-old Elizabeth tries to teach, however, is my little brother, Matthew. Everybody loves Matthew, even though he throws a lot of fits and pretty much breaks every rule in the house. He likes to draw on walls, cut his hair, and tear up our homework, but he also likes to randomly walk up to you, hug you, and say, "Mac, I wuv you," which pretty much makes up for all the other stuff he does.

So there you have it. That's my family. I like to complain about them, but really? They're not so bad. In fact, for most of my missions in life, they'd be my trusted allies. OPERATION SAVE THE SUMMER, however, is different.

I won't go so far as to call Mom an enemy. Frien-emy, maybe, or just "The Obstacle Which Must be Overcome."

The rest of the fam? I'll treat them with suspicion, for now.

Saturday, June 7, 7:30 p.m.

Dear Mission Diary,

I was right to treat the rest of the family with suspicion — especially Luke!

Today, he pointed out IN FRONT OF MOM that a "real" hunger strike would mean only drinking water — not milk or lemonade. So now I can't even drink milk at dinnertime while the rest of the family is eating.

To make matters worse, Mom served spaghetti tonight — another of my favorites.

"Come on, Mac. You're going to have to eat eventually," Mom said when I shook my head at the heaping pile of noodles she was about to put on my plate.

"I'll eat when I have Jerry back."

Mom dropped the spaghetti on Elizabeth's plate instead.

Dad chimed in, "I guess you'd better hurry up and finish your summer reading and journaling."

"Yes," Mom agreed. "Eventually, the lack of food will get to you. You'll be too weak to read or write."

Luke started laughing. Since he was in the

middle of taking a big swig from his glass,
milk spurted out of his nose.

Apparently, milk-spurting is kind of painful.
I wouldn't know, since — thanks to Luke — I
can't drink milk.

What I do know is watching my brother
howl in agony can be hilarious — especially
after he laughed at me!

Meanwhile, Clare was flipping out because
the milk flew straight from Luke's nose and
onto her food and Matthew decided it would
be funny to spit milk on her plate too, which
hardly helped matters.

Any concern Mom and Dad were beginning to show over my hunger strike was completely forgotten.

But here's the worst part: Once he recovered from the milk-spurting, Luke got seconds and then thirds on the spaghetti. I'm sure he did it on purpose. Now, there isn't any left, so I can't even sneak downstairs later to heat some up for myself.

Fortunately, I did manage to sneak more granola bars, plus half a bag of potato chips. I'll survive. The hunger strike is going strong.

At least, as far as Mom knows.

Sunday, June 8, 10:15 a.m.

Dear Mission Diary,

Okay, so maybe that stupid book Mom gave me isn't so bad. I started the first chapter when I went to bed last night and ended up reading until after midnight. I'm now 75 pages into it, which means I'm a quarter of the way done with summer reading. Plus, I've written 50 pages here, so I'm more than halfway to the goal on that count, too.

I'm still going to continue with the fake hunger strike, though, since I figure Mom will cave before too long. Seriously, she thinks I haven't eaten in five days!

The truth is, I don't feel very good. Pretty much all I've eaten in the last five days is donuts, granola bars, cookies, and potato chips, and I think that might be catching up with me.

Anyways, I probably won't make much progress on Operation Save the Summer today. We're going to church soon, and then after that we've got plans to hang out with the cousins. Even the most committed operative needs a day off every once in a while.

Dear Mission Diary,

Yesterday, I gained one more day of "hunger strike," but, really, I ate a TON.

First, there was Communion at church, which is surprisingly filling when you've eaten almost nothing for days. After that, we went to my aunt and uncle's house and they cooked hamburgers and hotdogs. All the food was in the kitchen, but all the people ate outside — which gave me plenty of time to chow down totally unobserved.

Not bad for my day off.

Dear Mission Diary,

Grayson from the house behind us came over today and told me he wants to save up to buy an electric scooter. With both of us being motivated to earn some cash, we decided to try doing another lemonade stand.

This time, though, we wanted to make more money. Elizabeth was at a friend's house, which meant we only had to split the profits two ways. Plus, we decided to add more products, since lemonade and cookies have limited income potential. I went through our bookshelves and found a ton of old kids' books no one ever reads and Grayson got a bunch of toys he doesn't play with anymore, which gave us a "lemonade, cookies, toys, and books stand."

We also decided to move the stand to the end of the street where there's a lot more traffic. It worked! Tons of people stopped. Some lady in a minivan bought a bunch of Grayson's toys and five of my books, plus lemonade and cookies for all her kids. AND, some lady stopped and gave us $5 for a single lemonade!

Each of us walked home with $26.

Now, THIS is progress!

Tuesday, June 10, 9:30 p.m.

Dear Mission Diary,

Today, Grayson asked if I could go with him to his grandparents' house. They live in the neighborhood next to ours, so Grayson rides his bike over there whenever he wants to.

Mom didn't like the idea at first, since I'd have to cross a busy street to get there. I finally talked her into it, but she insisted I wear a helmet. Since I didn't want to look like a total sissy, I took the dumb thing off and threw it under a bush as soon as we were out of sight of the house.

We made it to Grayson's grandparents' house, no problem. Grayson checked in with them and even grabbed me a much-needed ice cream sandwich from their freezer. Then we walked down to the creek that runs through their backyard and skipped rocks for a while. When that got boring, we took off our shoes and followed the creek until it went under a bridge that was too low for us to walk under.

Along the way, we did lots of cool stuff. I tried to catch a crawdad, but failed. We used a stick to dig into these snake-hole-looking things, but didn't find any snakes. We chased a bunch of frogs and even managed to catch a few. Grayson says you can fish in the creek, too, but we didn't have a fishing pole. Maybe next time.

We were there all afternoon, and traffic

was heavy when we rode home. I was riding along minding my own business when a car came zooming around the corner right at me. I swerved to avoid ending up on the front of the guy's car like a squashed bug. My tire hit the curb, I went flying over the handlebars, and landed head-first. Luckily, the grass cushioned my landing. I missed the concrete by less than an inch!

Mom always tells us to assume all drivers are idiots when we're riding our bikes. This guy was definitely an idiot, but I felt like the biggest idiot of all.

My head hurts like you wouldn't believe, and my back does, too. I'm not going to tell

Mom about it, though. She'd probably figure out I wasn't wearing that stupid helmet — which (okay, okay) I probably should have been wearing. Regardless, I'll bet she'd say I couldn't go to Grayson's grandparents again because the bike ride is too dangerous.

I'm a soldier in this battle, and soldiers have to be tough.

As far as Mom's concerned, I'm fine.

Still hungry, but just fine.

Wednesday, June 11, 12:25 p.m.

Dear Mission Diary,

I feel too horrible to do much of anything today. The bruise on the top of my skull is ginormous. My whole head is throbbing, and I can barely move my neck.

I did manage to search for Jerry while Mom took Matthew to a doctor's appointment this morning, but looking for stuff when you can barely move your head is incredibly difficult. I tried to go through the closets, but couldn't bend my neck to look up high. Instead I settled for Dad's dresser drawers. I was bent over, rooting around under a stack of shorts, when Mom walked in.

"Mac! What are you doing?"

I stood up really quick, but I had to turn my shoulders awkwardly so I could face her without moving my neck.

"Well, um, I'm ..."The pounding in my head made it hard to think, so I couldn't come up with a good excuse.

Mom crossed her arms over her chest. "Are you looking for that silly video game console?" she asked.

Apparently, the look on my face answered her question, because she just kept right on going. "Michael Anthony McMillan!"

She used my full name. I knew I was in serious trouble.

"This is an invasion of your father's privacy!"

"I'm sorry, I just—"

"You JUST were trying to find an easy way out of doing your summer reading and journaling."

I couldn't exactly deny that, so I kept my mouth shut.

"Too bad, buddy. Now you'll need to do more of both."

"WHAT??!!"

Mom held up a hand and gave me THE LOOK — the one that means, "arguing will only make it worse, so keep your trap shut."

"100 more pages of reading, Mac, and 50 more of journaling."

I stood there with my mouth gaping open. Mom kept talking. "The good news is, you'll have plenty of time to work on it, since you're grounded. Now, go get started."

I went to my room and tried to read for a little bit, but it made my head hurt. Come to think of it, writing makes my head hurt too. Plus, I'm starving — and I've run out of granola bars.

I guess I'll just take a nap.

Wednesday, June 11, 10:00 p.m.

Dear Mission Diary,

The nap helped my head, which was a good thing because life got a little crazy during dinner.

I was trying not to think about how good the crescent rolls smelled when Luke said, "Mom, my head itches."

Mom sat there. Luke sat there. They looked at each other, and we all knew that this could only mean one thing.

"I'll go get a towel," Luke volunteered.

This has happened before. He knows the drill.

We ALL know the drill.

Mom pushed her chair back from the table, stood up, and went to gather her supplies.

Her plate was still on the table, nearly full.

I looked at that plate for a long time, mouth watering. Dad was still sitting there, though, so I didn't dare grab a fork and dive in like I wanted to. Instead, I went into the kitchen to watch the drama unfold.

Mom pulled a chair into the middle of the kitchen, and Luke sat down, towel wrapped around his shoulders. Mom took the spray bottle filled with olive oil and sprayed it all over Luke's head until his hair was one big grease-slick. Then she took the little red-handled lice comb and pulled it through Luke's hair. She wiped the comb on a paper towel, took a deep breath, and used her fingernail to squish the tiny bug she must've found.

Mom stood there for a long time, breathing

in through her nose and out through her mouth, not saying a word.

Luke finally broke the silence. "Mom?"

"Yes, Luke."

"Do I have lice?"

"Yes, Luke."

"So, what are you doing?"

Duh. Mom does one of two things in a situation like this:

1.) Totally flips out and starts running around like a madwoman, yelling at everybody to strip their sheets, vacuum every crevice, and — for the love of all that's good! — don't put your head on anything! (That's what she did last time Luke had lice.)

— or —

2.) Practices deep breathing exercises while praying for patience and the death of all lice — or whatever it is Mom prays for at times like these.

Of course, some people need to have things spelled out.

"I'm praying, Luke," Mom said.

She took one last deep breath and started combing through Luke's hair again.

Since any intelligent human knows when it's best to flee a crisis, I began to back slowly out of the kitchen.

"Don't go far, Mac. You've got to be checked, too."

I groaned. Getting checked for lice is awful.

And then I groaned again. Getting checked for lice with a giant secret bruise on my head was going to be even worse!

"But Mom! My head doesn't itch!"

"You know how this works, Mac. Everybody has to be checked."

"But I've never had lice! I shouldn't have to get checked!"

"Yeah, Mom," Luke chimed in. "Lice like clean hair, and we all know Mac's hair isn't clean. There's no way he has lice."

I wasn't about to argue with his logic. Instead, I headed to my room and hoped Mom would forget I even existed — at least until the lice-checking was over.

I stopped thinking about lice real fast, though, when I walked into my room and saw a giant ant climbing up the ladder of my bed.

"MOM!" I yelled. "THERE'S AN ANT ON MY BED!"

She didn't answer, so I went to the top of the stairs and yelled it again.

"MAC!" she finally yelled back, and I knew that she'd forgotten about the whole deep-breathing-exercise-while-praying-thing. "I'M BUSY KILLING LICE! YOU'LL HAVE TO TAKE CARE OF THE ANT YOURSELF!"

I went back to my room, grabbed a tennis ball off the floor, and used it to smash the ant. Then I threw the ball over to Luke's side of the room.

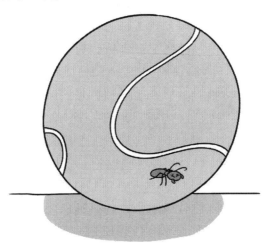

Problem solved, or so I thought. When I went back to the ladder, though, there was ANOTHER huge ant on it. I went and got a stool so I could look into my bed without getting on the ladder, and I counted EIGHT ants crisscrossing the sheet.

I ran down the stairs and into the kitchen, yelling Mom's name the whole way. "There are ants all over my bed!"

Mom didn't say anything. Just closed her eyes and took one of her deep breaths.

Luke wasn't so quiet. "Dude! I'll come kill 'em for you!"

Finally, Mom said in a soft voice, "Luke, you need to sit here until I'm done pulling bugs from your hair. Then, please feel free to kill as many ants as you like. However, we'll need to figure out what is attracting them to Mac's bed."

"Hmmm, I wonder what that could be?"

Luke said, a wicked grin all over his face.

"I don't know! I just want them out of my bed! And then I want clean sheets!"

I waited while Mom finished combing through Luke's hair, which took forever. And then, of course, she insisted she had to check MY hair before she'd go look at the ants. With each pass, pain arced through my entire brain and exploded behind my eyes. It was all I could do to hold back the screams every time that evil comb scraped over the knot on my head.

I swear Mom must've combed over that bruise 13 trillion times. Finally, I wadded up the end of the towel so I could bite down on it instead of screaming.

"Mac, is there something wrong with your head right here?" she asked, pressing a finger into my scalp.

I jumped off the chair. "OW! OW! OW! OW! OW!"

Mom was all sweetness now. "I'm sorry, honey!" she cried. "What happened?"

"I—I—I must have hit it on something," I managed to strangle out.

She made me sit back down and finish the lice check, but she said she'd probably covered that area enough. Luckily, it wasn't long before she declared me lice-free.

"Ha!" Luke laughed. "That proves that lice don't like dirty hair!"

"I'd rather have dirty hair than bugs

crawling in it!" I told him. "And, besides, you're just jealous 'cause you have to get checked for lice again tomorrow!"

"You'll have to be checked again in a few days, too," Mom reminded me. "Just to be safe."

Every few days is better than every day, so I didn't complain.

Luke and I headed upstairs to kill some ants while Mom checked Elizabeth's hair. As soon as we got to our room, Luke grabbed a Nerf bullet from the floor and climbed the ladder.

"Die!" he yelled as he smashed an ant under the bullet's head.

I grabbed the ladder from Luke's bed and hooked it to my bed so I could climb up and watch his progress.

"Die!" he smashed another. "Die!" And another. "Die!" And another.

The only problem was, no matter how many he killed, more ants kept appearing. "Dude, you've got a serious problem here," Luke informed me after he'd killed about a bazillion.

"Duh!" I yelled. I jumped off the ladder and grabbed a bullet of my own.

Just then, Mom appeared in the doorway. She watched us assaulting the herd of ants for a minute before taking over.

"Alright, boys, let's see what we're dealing with here." She shooed Luke off my ladder and climbed up several rungs.

She pulled the sheet back.

The granola bar wrappers I'd hidden at the bottom of my bed appeared. Only, they were so covered in ants, they actually MOVED! It was like they'd come to life!

Mom and I both jumped off our ladders and away from the bed. "That's all you, Mac," Mom said. She put an arm around my shoulder.

"What?!"

"You know you're not supposed to have food in your room. This is why. It's all you. Get it cleaned up."

"But Mom! There are ants EVERYWHERE!"

"Yep, there are." She squeezed my shoulder. "And you're going to clean them up." She turned and walked toward the doorway, then turned back around to smile at me. "Nice hunger strike, by the way."

Back to the drawing board on the mission plan. First, though, I had to deal with the ants.

Luke helped me strip the blanket and sheets, being careful to contain the ants inside. We crammed them into a trash bag, tied it off, and put it in the garage so the ants would suffocate. Then we got bug spray and sprayed all around the baseboards. Hopefully no more ants will come in looking for granola bar crumbs!

Sometimes, having an older brother isn't so bad — even if he does get lice all the time.

Thursday, June 12, 8:30 a.m.

Dear Mission Diary,

Everything I've done to get Jerry back has failed. The cover is blown on my hunger strike, plus it gave me ants. Trying to find Jerry just got me stuck doing more reading and journaling, and I'm STILL grounded. Not to mention that I'm a LONG way from earning enough money to buy a new console.

I tried to be nice, but desperate times call for desperate measures. There's one thing I haven't attempted yet ...

I haven't tried reporting Mom to the police for child neglect.

If all goes well, I will get Jerry back TODAY.

Here goes.

Thursday, June 12, 4:30 p.m.

Dear Mission Diary,

That didn't go well.

Dear Mac's (Stupid)
Mission Diary,

Mac is an idiot. A total,
complete IDIOT. I'm writing
it here so MAYBE he can
remember what an IDIOT
he is, and never do anything
so IDIOTIC again.

The dude used MY PHONE
to call THE POLICE and
REPORT MOM FOR CHILD
NEGLECT.

I caught him before he
even managed to finish the
sentence, "I'm calling to
report my mom for child
neglect," but it was too
late.

DUDE!! Mac!! THERE REALLY ARE KIDS WHO ARE NEGLECTED. YOU ARE NOT ONE OF THEM. MOM FEEDS YOU (when you choose to eat.) SHE KEEPS A ROOF OVER YOUR HEAD (which you infest with ants.) SHE LOVES YOU (even though you're a total idiot.)

SAVE THE 911 CALL FOR A REAL EMERGENCY.

DON'T FORGET: YOU ARE AN IDIOT.

Your Much Smarter Brother,

Luke

Thursday, June 12, 4:55 p.m.

Dear Mission Diary,

So, yeah. I called 911 on Mom. Luke threw a tennis ball at my head and stopped me. It was the same tennis ball I killed the ant with.

I guess he's right. Video game deprivation does not actually count as child neglect.

Fake hunger strikes don't, either.

Even ant-infested beds don't count, so long as your mom provides another, clean place to sleep.

Ask me how I know.

Go ahead. Ask.

Yeah, that's right.

About ten minutes after Luke threw the ant-guts-covered tennis ball at my face, the doorbell rang. And then, a couple minutes later, Mom came upstairs and told me I had a visitor. I thought maybe it was Grayson wanting to hang out, and this was just Mom's way of torturing me by making me tell him I was grounded. No such luck.

I guess once you call 911 they have to follow up and make sure everything's okay.

"Young man, did you call 911?"

(Gulp)

"Yes, sir."

"Can you tell me why, son?"

"I, um, wanted to report my mom for child neglect. Sir."

The officer looked at Mom. "Ma'am, would there be a safe place where I could talk to your son alone for a moment?"

"Yes, officer. Why don't you two sit on the front porch? You'll have privacy there," Mom said.

I followed the cop outside and sat down in one of the big wooden chairs that always make me feel like a total midget. If I wasn't already feeling about two feet tall, that definitely did the trick. My eyes filled up with embarrassing tears, but I managed to wipe them away before the guy noticed.

The cop sat down in the other chair and hunched forward. He told me his name and I told him mine. He said he had a nephew about my age who liked to play basketball, and did I like to play basketball? Then he looked me square in the eye and got real serious.

"Mac, who do you feel is being neglected? Is it you, or one of your siblings?"

"Me," I croaked.

"And can you tell me how you're being neglected?"

Suddenly, I realized how stupid it was going to sound. I said it anyway. "My mom took away Jerr— I mean, my gaming console."

The officer raised an eyebrow.

79

"But my brother heard me calling 911, and he stopped me. I realize now that it's probably not really child neglect."

"No, son, taking away your console is definitely not child neglect. In fact, I think your mom limiting your video games is one way she shows she cares about you."

I nodded, even though I'm not sure I believe that.

Next, he asked, "Is there anything else that's making you feel neglected?"

"Well, I went on a hunger strike for eight days, and Mom didn't stop me."

"Did she make food available to you?"

"Yes."

"Did you honestly not eat for eight days?"

"Well, um, I ate some granola bars, and a banana, and a couple cheeseburgers, and some cookies and I drank some lemonade, and—"

"So, you ate plenty."

"Well, I was definitely hungry a lot."

"That's not child neglect, young man."

I nodded. "I know that now, sir."

"Anything else?"

"Um, there were ants in my bed?"

"Did you have a clean place to sleep, that didn't have ants?

"Uh-huh."

"Still not child neglect." He leaned forward and looked me in the eye. "Look, buddy. I'm willing to bet your mom has very good reasons for taking away your video games."

I shrugged.

"And I'll bet she loves you very much."

I shrugged again and wished those stupid tears would stop trying to come.

"So, I think you'd probably better go in there and tell your mom you're sorry."

"Yes, sir. I will, sir."

He stood up and opened the door for me. I felt even shorter than I did when I sat in that dumb chair. Mom was in the kitchen, and came into the foyer when she heard us at the door. I tried to hold them back, but the tears started flowing again.

"I'm sorry, Mom."

She came over and wrapped her arms around me. "I forgive you, Mac."

Mom left her arm around my shoulder while she and the cop talked for a few minutes. Once he left, she sat me down and gave me a long lecture about how Jerry is too important to me and I need to get my priorities straight. Then she told me that since I wasted the officer's time, I was going to have to do community service to make it up.

"Community service?! He didn't say anything about community service!"

"No, he didn't, Mac, but I think it's a reasonable consequence for calling the police without cause."

"But what do I have to do?"

"Well, when I took Elizabeth and Matthew to the park the other day, I noticed a lot of trash laying around. I figure you can clean it up."

"What?! Mom, that's not fair."

She didn't even bother to respond. Just squeezed my shoulder, raised her eyebrows at me, and went back to the kitchen.

Thursday, June 12, 8:55 p.m.

Dear Mission Diary,

One good thing happened today: I ate dinner. Mom made fried chicken with mashed potatoes, biscuits, green beans, and applesauce.

It was pretty much the best meal I've ever eaten.

Friday, June 13, 9:00 p.m.

Dear Mission Diary,

Mom took me to Holliday Park today to do my community service. She sent Matthew and Elizabeth off to play on the playground, handed me a pair of garden gloves and a trash bag, sat down on a park bench with a book, and told me to get to work.

I picked up all the trash I saw around her park bench, and told her I was done.

"What about that?" She waved a finger at a bush on the other side of the sidewalk.

"I don't see any trash there."

"Oh, I do. Look under the bush."

I had to get down on my hands and knees and reach under the stupid bush to get a cup some jerk didn't bother to put in a trash can. Once I'd done that, she pointed to a bunch of flowers that had old newspaper wrapped around their stems. This went on for a long time, but the worst part was right after I had finally managed to wrestle a dirty diaper from underneath a bush.

There I was, on my knees, trash bag in one hand and dirty diaper in the other, when two kids from my class at school — Brent and Alex — came walking up.

"Dude, what're you doing?" Alex asked, already laughing at me.

"Well, I'm—" I looked at the diaper, and then at the trash bag, and tried to think of a reasonable explanation.

"Is that a DIAPER?" Brent asked, scrunching up his nose. He was tossing a basketball from one hand to the other.

"Yes, well, um—" I scrambled up so at least I wasn't crawling around on the ground anymore, "—I'm doing my part for the community," I finally said lamely.

"Way to go. Good deed done," Brent said,

and he tossed the basketball to me. "Want to come shoot some hoops with us?"

I dropped the diaper but caught the ball. "Yeah, that'd be cool—" I looked at Mom, who raised her eyebrows and pointed to a bush that had a dirty tissue caught in its limbs, "—after I finish this." I tried to say it as if crawling around Holliday Park and cleaning up trash was exactly what I wanted to be doing on a summer afternoon.

I passed the ball back to Brent, and they headed to the basketball courts without a backwards glance. I returned to litter-cleaning duty and argued with myself over whether I should go play basketball with them once I was done or go home and try to pretend the whole thing never happened.

Since basketball is the sport I'm best at, I decided to use my very respectable skills to redeem my reputation. Of course, technically, I'm still grounded, but Mom apparently forgot that briefly and said "yes" when I asked if I could go play.

Alex and Brent were playing a game of one-on-one when I finally arrived at the court. Since we'd have uneven teams, we decided to play HORSE, which I knew I could win. Sure enough, Brent had H-O-R, Alex had H-O-R-S, and I only had H when we got to talking about what we'd been doing so far this summer. Brent and Alex's pretty much revolved around video games, especially since a new game just came out last week.

"Dude, I held the world-wide top score for an hour on Tuesday," Brent bragged.

"Whatever, bro," Alex said, "I beat your top score on Wednesday, but Gameboy Brad took over and now nobody can beat him."

They talked for a while about which weapons are best, the best hiding places, and stuff like that. Of course, I barely even knew the game existed, so I had nothing to add to the conversation.

Eventually, they realized I hadn't said anything. "What about you, Mac? I haven't seen you on the boards," Brent said.

"Yeah, I haven't been playing," I said, trying to act all cool. "My buddy's grandparents live on Williams Creek, and we've been hanging out there, hunting snakes and catching frogs and stuff." I was going to suggest they come see it, until Brent laughed.

"Dude, that sounds pretty lame," he said and rolled his eyes.

Alex laughed too. Then he flapped his wrist in front of his chest and sang, "I wike to go to da cweek and catch fwoggies."

It was my turn to take a shot. I went all the way to the edge of the court. *SWISH*.

Alex was up next.

Ka-chunk.

Game over. I won. Take that, Mister-I-Wike-to-Catch-Fwoggies-Jerk!

We kept shooting around for a little bit, and I continued to prove my superiority in basketball, no matter who has the highest score on their stupid new video game.

Finally, I saw Elizabeth running towards the court and knew it was time to go. I took one last shot, another *swish*, and caught the ball after it flowed like water through the net.

"Hey, you should log on when you get home so we can play a game or two together," Brent said as he waited for me to throw him the ball.

"I can't," I admitted, and I did the trick where I pass the ball behind my back and catch it. "My mom took my console until I finish my summer reading and do a bunch of writing stuff."

"Dude, seriously?" Alex acted like it was the worst thing in the world. Which it is, or I mean, I used to think it was. Now, though . . .

I shrugged. "Yeah. I thought it was pretty awful at first, too, but now I realize—" I took a deep breath and remembered Alex flapping his wrist and making fun of catching fwoggies. "—video games make people boring."

Just at that moment, Elizabeth reached the court and yelled that we were leaving. I tossed the ball to Brent, waved, and took off.

Saturday, June 14, 8:45 p.m.

Dear Mission Diary,

Since I finally got ungrounded today, Grayson and I went to his grandparents' to hang out at the creek. On our way there, though, the street was blocked by a huge tree that had fallen across it.

We were discussing whether we should try to haul our bikes over the tree or go around the block to avoid it when a man came up carrying a chain saw—which would have been super scary, except there was a fallen tree right in front of us.

"Hi, boys," chainsaw man said. "You'll probably want to go around the block to get around this. It'll be a while before we get the road cleared."

While the guy was talking, Justin Adams came up and stood beside him wearing work gloves. Justin's a grade above me at school, but he's always been nice, even though he's definitely in the "cool group" of seventh-graders.

"Hey," he said, "how do you like our tree?"

"Nice," I laughed, "but it's kind of in a bad location."

"Tell me about it," Justin rolled his eyes. "At least it's not in front of your house, so you don't have to be the one to help clean it up."

I couldn't have agreed more, but then Grayson said, "We can help!"

Suddenly my chance to have fun appeared to be crashing down just like that tree had.

Justin was all about having some help, and chainsaw man — apparently his dad — agreed. "That would be great, boys," he said. "With extra hands, we'll make quick work of it."

I tried to think of a way out of it. I had already done plenty of community service yesterday. I wasn't too excited about doing more. Before I could come up with a good excuse, though, Justin had gone to get work gloves for us, his dad had started cutting limbs, and Grayson was hauling them to the side of the road.

As it turned out, the job wasn't so bad. Some of their neighbors came and helped, and we had that tree totally cleaned up in less than a half hour. Plus, after we were done Justin went into his house and came back with popsicles for each of us.

Grayson doesn't go to my school, so he wasn't aware of the fact that Justin is older and too cool to want to come to the geeky creek with us. "Hey," he said while we were peeling off the wrappers, "we were on our way to the creek behind my grandparents' house. Do you want to come with us?"

I about dropped my popsicle in embarrassment, but then Justin said, "That'd be awesome!" and went to ask his dad.

So, it ended up being three of us that went to Grayson's grandparents' house. We walked up and down the creek, just like we'd done the first day we explored, and Justin said the spot where the creek goes underneath the bridge would be perfect for a fort. Technically, it's on somebody else's property, but Grayson's grandparents texted the owners and they said they were out of town and it was fine by them.

We hauled a bunch of firewood from Grayson's grandpa's woodpile, and used it to build a wall running up the bank. Between the firewood-wall, the bridge, and the bank, the fort is protected on three sides. Only the creek-side is open.

We went back to Justin's house, got three big chunks of the tree that had fallen, and hauled them back to the creek in his little brother's wagon so we could use them as stools. Then, we dangled our feet in the water while we discussed our plans to make the fort even cooler.

It was almost dinner-time when I finally got home. I sat down on the couch and noticed that the cat was sleeping under the TV, right where Jerry should have been.

You know what?

I didn't even care.

Dear Mission Diary,

Grayson and I met up with Justin yesterday afternoon like we planned, plus Justin brought his friend Pete Larson along. We ended up being there most of the day, and only took a break to have lunch at Justin's house. We built the walls even higher and dug out part of the bank to make a dirt chair.

Then we raided Grayson's grandparents' garage and found a bunch of great stuff which they said we could use. We covered the dirt chair with an old picnic-table tablecloth, and we set up two beach umbrellas for shade. Grayson even figured out a way to build a couple of shelves into the log wall, and we hung a hammock between two nearby trees.

When we were done, I called Mom from Justin's house to see if they could all spend the night. She said no at first, because she's still freaked out about someone catching lice. But I asked if we could sleep outside in the tent. I could hardly believe it, but she said yes!

Just when you thought there was no upside to your brother having lice, your sleepover turns into a campout and it's totally cool.

95

Dad built a fire and we cooked hot dogs and made s'mores. I'm so glad I'm not on that stupid fake hunger strike anymore! After s'mores, we played ghost in the graveyard and caught lightning bugs, and then we took turns telling scary stories around the fire.

Grayson brought over an air mattress and we played rock, paper, scissors to decide who got to sleep on it. I was one of the winners, but the thing kept losing air, so we constantly had to wake up to re-inflate it.

I figure it was around two in the morning when we all woke up because we heard something rustling around outside the tent. With all the scary stories we'd told, we got pretty freaked out and thought about going inside. That meant facing whatever was out there, though, so we decided to just stay inside the tent. Maybe it was just a raccoon. Or maybe it was Sasquatch. I wasn't about to find out.

It took forever, but we finally fell back to sleep, only to wake up when all the birds started chirping their heads off. We contemplated throwing rocks at them to shut them up, but finally decided to just jump on the trampoline instead.

After breakfast, we wanted to go back
to the creek, but Mom said I had to do my
chores. Once those were done, I went back
to bed. Sleeping in a tent is cool, but it felt
awfully good to crawl into my own bed. I was
so tired, I don't think I'd have even noticed if
the ants were back.

Dear Mission Diary,

Grayson, Justin, and I met up again today and decided to ride our bikes over to the park to play basketball. On our way, we saw Alex sitting in front of his house looking bored out of his mind — like maybe that new video game isn't so much fun, after all.

Despite my best efforts to distract Grayson and Justin, Alex managed to flag us down. When he asked where we were going, I tried to give Justin the look that says, "He's a total jerk, don't tell him!" Justin didn't notice, though, and — nice guy that he is — he invited Alex to go to the park and play basketball with us.

We played a game of two-on-two, me and Grayson against Justin and Alex. Justin's a pretty good basketball player, plus he's older, so I was sure they would beat us. As it turns out though, Grayson's a genius at basketball. Plus, Alex couldn't make a shot to save his life.

When I made the game-winning shot, Alex got all ticked off. He grabbed the ball and threw it into the bushes. We all lit into him for throwing a temper tantrum and told him he had to go get the ball. He couldn't reach it without climbing in between the limbs, though, and he got all freaked out because he saw a few spider webs.

I couldn't help it. I started laughing. "Dude, you're afraid of a spider web?"

"I don't like spiders!" he yelled back before adding, "Why don't you come and get the ball, if you like bugs so much?"

It was the perfect opening for me to give him a hard time after his comment about me catching fwoggies, so I said, "I don't like bugs so much. I just like the animals that eat them. Remember?"

The blank stare on Alex's face made it obvious he had no idea what I was talking about.

"I 'wike to go to da cweek and catch fwoggies,' right?" I joked. "That's what you said, at least!"

Alex just stood there still looking stupid, but Justin and Grayson began to understand what was going on.

"Dude, did you make fun of Mac for hanging out at the creek?" Justin asked Alex.

Alex shrugged and looked uncomfortable. "It sounded totally lame," he said.

Justin had walked over to the bushes and climbed right through those spider webs, no problem. "You don't know what lame is," he said as he tossed the ball out to Alex.

Alex caught the ball. "Yeah, well, maybe it's not so bad. It just sounded really stupid at the time."

I shrugged. "Well, guys," I directed to Justin and Grayson. "You ready to go check on the fort?"

"Yep!" they both answered.

"Fort?" Alex perked up all of a sudden. "I built a super cool fort! It's got eight stories, and a hot tub, and a TV, and—"

"Bro, our fort's not in a stupid video game!" Justin laughed.

Grayson laughed too, "Dude, this is a real fort. We built it with dirt and logs." There was a challenge in his voice, like he was daring

Alex to try to compete with THAT.

"A real fort? Where did you build a real fort?"

"At the creek," I answered. "You wouldn't want to come, though. The creek is lame, right?"

Alex just kept standing there with his mouth hanging wide open. Me, Justin, and Grayson hopped on our bikes, waved goodbye, and headed to the fort.

Wednesday, June 18, 4:45 p.m.

Dear Mission Diary,

When Mom came upstairs to tell me goodnight last night, I told her about that whole thing with Alex. She said we weren't very nice to him and that I should try to rectify the situation. I didn't know what "rectify" meant, but I looked it up. Basically, it means I need to make things right.

I thought about it for a long time while I was trying to fall asleep, and I had to admit that mom had a point. I was just as mean to Alex as he and Brent had been to me, maybe even more, since it was three of us to one kid, instead of just two to one. Plus, even after they were jerks to me, Brent and Alex asked about playing video games together. We just took off and left Alex on the basketball court by himself.

I talked to Mom about it this morning and she said I should go over to Alex's house, apologize, and ask him if he wanted to go see the fort. I totally didn't want to do that, but Mom insisted that it was the right thing to do and that I'd feel better once I did it.

I almost turned around three times on the way there, and I had that stupid prickly nervous feeling in my hands again when I rang the doorbell. But by then there was no

102

turning back.

Alex answered the door, game controller in his hand.

"Hey," he said. The universal kids' greeting.

"Hey." Now that I was there, I realized I hadn't fully thought through what I was going to say. I inspected my gym shoes for a few seconds before I finally looked up and said, "I'm sorry about yesterday."

Alex shrugged. "It's okay. I guess I kind of had it coming. I'm sorry I was rude to you the other day."

I couldn't argue with that, so I just said, "You can come see the fort if you want."

"I'm playing with Brent right now."

"Oh, is he here?" I asked, suddenly embarrassed that maybe he'd heard my apology.

"No, he's at his house." Alex held up the controller.

Funny how being away from video games for a couple of weeks makes me think playing "with" a kid means you're actually in the same building.

"Okay. Well, if you change your mind, we're headed there in a little bit."

"Sure. Thanks." Alex stepped backward and started to close the door. "Well, I gotta go," he said. "I've probably missed a whole game already."

Mom was right. I definitely felt better about things as I rode my bike home. I was bummed out for Alex, though, and I still kind of am. He doesn't know what he's missing.

Thursday, June 19, 9:35 p.m.

Dear Mission Diary,

Justin is a genius.

The kid that lives next door to him wanted to come see our fort.

"Sure, we'd be happy to show it to you," Justin said, "for five bucks."

I guess this kid's parents pay him a ginormous allowance or something, because he didn't even think twice, just yelled "okay!" and ran back to his house.

"Wait a minute!" Justin yelled after him. The kid stopped and turned back around.

"Five bucks is for the basic tour. If you want the deluxe tour, it'll be ten."

"What's included in the deluxe tour?" the kid asked.

"Ice cream sandwiches and root beer, plus you can hang out in the fort for a half hour to eat them."

The kid shrugged, went into his house, and came back with ten bucks!

"You got any friends that'll want to come, too?" Justin asked him.

The kid thought for a minute. "Yeah, my cousin lives a few blocks over and he'd probably like to go, and I'll bet my friend Danny would, too."

An hour later, we had a crew of eight kids, all wanting to see the fort. A few of them only had five bucks, so they didn't get the deluxe package, but STILL! After that, we put up signs all over both neighborhoods, and Justin and Grayson messaged their friends through their gaming consoles. I couldn't believe the number of kids who wanted to come see our fort!

One kid just got a bunch of money for his birthday, so he paid us 40 bucks to let him and a couple of his friends hang out there for an hour!

By the end of the day, we'd each made $60. With the money I already had from lemonade stands, plus the allowance Mom finally paid me, I'm up to $125.61!!

Friday, June 20, 9:35 p.m.

Dear Mission Diary,

As it turns out, Grayson's a genius, too — and not just at basketball.

He has two video game consoles: One at his mom's house, and one at his dad's.

With all the money we've made from the lemonade stand and the fort tours, he's less than $100 away from being able to buy that electric scooter he wants. Last night he was trying to figure out how he could make the rest of the money, and he came up with a brilliant idea:

HE'S GOING TO SELL ONE OF HIS CONSOLES TO ME!!!!!!

Of course, I've only got $125.61, and the console's worth more than that, but he said I could pay him the rest once I get it. That shouldn't be too long, since Mom told me she's got yard work she'll pay me to do. Plus, she's willing to pay me to play with Matthew so she can work.

This mission is nearly complete!

Dear Mission Diary,

Harry's home.

Yep. You got it. Jerry's brother, whom I have officially named Harry, is right where he should be.

Of course, you can't really see him because I've devised a way to hide him behind the TV stand when he's not in use. That way, Mom won't know I have him. But, trust me, he's there. I got him all hooked up, and even had a few minutes to play while Mom was gone today. It was almost as good as eating fried chicken at the end of a fake hunger strike.

Sunday, June 22, 8:30 p.m.

Dear Mission Diary,

Grayson came over after church today and wanted to go to the creek. Mom was gone, though, so that wasn't an option. I had to take advantage of her absence to play video games.

When she got home, I went over to Grayson's house to see if he still wanted to go to the creek, but he wasn't there. I jumped on the trampoline for a little bit and read my book, which I'm actually super close to finishing. All in all, though, today ended up being incredibly boring, even if I did get to play video games for a while.

Monday, June 23, 12:23 p.m.

Dear Mission Diary,

I'm in major trouble.

Mom said she'd pay me to watch Matthew
this morning so she could get caught up on
work. I agreed, of course, because I still owe
Grayson a ton of money.

So then she told me she'd be in her office,
and that we shouldn't disturb her unless
we were bleeding profusely or vomiting
uncontrollably.

That's when I realized: Mom wasn't coming
out of her office any time soon. It was the
perfect time to play games on Harry.

Things were going really well. Matthew sat

beside me for a while and watched me play. I even gave him the other controller and let him think he was playing, which he was totally into at first.

But then he lost interest and went into Clare and Elizabeth's room. I heard him rummaging around in there, but I didn't care. I was in the zone and on a roll. When he came back into the room with Elizabeth's latest slime concoction, I noticed that it was turning his hands red, but I didn't care. I was THIS CLOSE to hitting a new personal record.

I lost that game just shy of that PR, so I started another, determined that today was going to be the day I'd hit the international high-score board. Sweat beaded my lip and my hands shook slightly as I passed my PR and edged closer and closer to the all-time-record.

I was preparing to make a sniper shot at an unsuspecting foe when I heard Mom yelling my name.

It wasn't the "Mac, you've got a friend at the door" yell.

It wasn't even the "MAC! The toilet's overflowing, hurry up and get the plunger!" yell.

THIS yell was a yell I'd never heard before, which I can now call the "MAC!!! Your little brother has destroyed the house and I might just kill you!" yell.

I threw the controller down, but then I hesitated. Should I wait and see if maybe she'd remember to practice the stop-breathe-pray exercise? I stayed where I was for a second, but then she yelled my name again. And again. And again. By then I knew we were way past stop-breathe-pray.

Experience told me the best thing I could do was run to Mom like the house was on fire, which I did. When I reached the family room, though, I wished I'd just run out of the house — like it really was on fire. The color of Mom's face perfectly matched Matthew's bright-red hands, which were busy trying to wipe away the tears streaming down his face. Matthew's hair — what was left of it, at least — was caked with bright red slime.

"What happ— "

"Matthew got your sister's slime," Mom said.

I nodded. "I see that."

"And he got it in his hair."

"I see that, too."

"And then he tried to cut it out of his hair."

"Oh, that makes sense."

"And while he was cutting his hair, he put the slime down." Mom looked at the carpet around her feet. "On the carpet."

"Oh.".

"Yes, oh," Mom echoed.

I took a step backwards and realized my sock was wet. I lifted my foot and set it back down with a squish.

I was afraid to ask, but I had to know. "So, why is the carpet wet?" My voice was literally a squeak.

Mom pointed to the little coffee bar on one side of the family room. The sink was full of water, and water was dripping from the counter onto the floor.

"He turned on the faucet so he could clean up the slime," Mom didn't even look at me. Just stared at the water drip-drip-dripping from the coffee bar. "What he didn't realize, apparently, was that the drain was closed."

Suddenly, I wished the water was deeper, so it would just cover me up and I could maybe swim away.

"I'll clean it up, Mom," I promised instead.

"But you can't clean up slime with water."

115

Mom's voice got higher and louder. "In fact, you can't clean up slime at all!"

Finally, Mom turned to look me in the eye.

"WHERE WERE YOU???!!!"

I didn't answer.

"WHAT WERE YOU DOING???!!!"

I just stood there, afraid to say anything, wishing the floor would swallow me whole.

"WHERE WERE YOU?" Mom yelled, as if the answer might somehow dry the carpet, remove the slime, and regrow Matthew's hair. Which it wouldn't, of course.

I thought about pointing that out but Mom started yelling again before I could.

"YOUR BROTHER FOUND THE SLIME, GOT IT INTO HIS HAIR, TRIED TO CUT IT OUT, TRIED TO CLEAN THE CARPET, AND FLOODED THE FAMILY ROOM! WHERE—"

All of a sudden Mom stopped, like she'd suddenly remembered something. She shut her mouth and closed her eyes. She breathed in through her nose. She breathed out through her mouth. And I breathed, too, for the first time in what felt like forever.

Mom kept breathing, and I came up with an angle. "Elizabeth isn't supposed to leave her slime where Matthew can reach it," I pointed out.

Mom opened her eyes and looked straight into mine.

"Where were you?" she asked quietly.

Somehow, the chill in her voice made me feel way worse than the heat had before.

"I was in the hangout room," I squeaked.

"The hangout room." Mom said it quietly, but somehow made it sound like I'd committed a felony offense. "What were you doing in the hangout room?" she asked.

I didn't answer. Matthew did.

"Mac was pwaying video games."

Mom looked at me for a long time, then closed her eyes. She breathed in through her nose, but the air whooshed right back out. The sound made me imagine a dragon preparing to breathe fire all over its helpless victim.

No fire came out, though. Mom nodded her head, pursed her lips, and walked right past me — squish, squash, squish through the wet carpet — toward the stairs.

I stayed where I was and considered my next move. I could wrap Matthew up in sponges, then roll him around on the floor to sop up the water.

I could turn the water back on, grab some floaties and convince Mom to turn the family room into an indoor pool.

I could grab the last of the granola bars, my toothbrush, and a pillow, and move into the fort by the creek.

I could—

Suddenly, Mom was standing in front of me holding my precious new Harry.

"Clean this up," she said in a quiet voice, and I knew the pool wasn't going to work out. "Once you're done, you can go to your room. We'll talk later."

I used every towel in the house to soak the water out of the carpet, but it's still sopping wet. Mom was right about the slime, too. I've tried everything Google could recommend, and the stain's still there.

So, now I've been in my room for over an hour and she still hasn't come for that little "talk" she promised. My hand is killing me from all this writing, but I'm too worried to relax. What's she going to do? Make me clean up trash at the dirtiest, nastiest park in town?

Ground me for the rest of my life?

Make me read a bazillion pages and write a thousand more?

Force me to clean toilets until I go to college?

Speculation is useless, I guess. I'm going to give my hand a break and go try to take a nap.

Dear Mission Diary,

Game over. Mission failed.

Mom proved herself a worthy adversary, and, ultimately, I have to admit that she was generous in victory.

When she finally walked into my room last night, she surprised me by giving me a hug and telling me she was sorry.

"What do YOU have to be sorry for? I'm the one that didn't watch Matthew," I said.

"True," she agreed, "but I shouldn't have lost my temper and yelled at you. For that, I apologize."

I sat there thinking that I should probably apologize, too, but the words seemed to be stuck somewhere in my throat.

"Look, Mac," Mom said, "you know you screwed up, and you know there have to be consequences."

I nodded my head without looking at her.

"Leaving a four-year-old unattended is stupid, and down-right dangerous. Matthew could have been hurt."

Again, I nodded.

"Your punishment will be three-fold. First, you'll need to practice better responsibility by watching Matthew every morning for the next two weeks."

I grimaced, but didn't argue.

"Secondly, you'll need to pay to repair the damage that was done. Matthew needs a new haircut, for starters, and the carpet . . . well, your dad and I agree that we need to have it dried out and cleaned by professionals. That'll cost several hundred dollars."

"Mom! I don't have that much money!" I said — and I confessed about still owing Grayson money for Harry.

"Well, that's a bummer," she agreed, "but I know just how you can earn the money to pay Grayson back, AND pay for the carpet."

I stared at her, calculating the numbers

in my head. By the time I paid Grayson back AND paid for everything else, it was going to be three or four hundred dollars, at least!

"You'll earn the money by doing yard work, cleaning house, and ..." she paused until I finally looked her in the eyes "... selling your gaming consoles."

"What??!!!"

"You heard me," Mom said. "You're overly attached to those games, and it's not healthy for you. So, you can sell the one you purchased from Grayson, as well as the one you already had."

"But what about Luke, Clare, and Elizabeth? It's theirs, too," I pointed out.

Mom just shrugged. "They barely use it. They'll be fine. And you can help them with their chores or something to compensate them for their share of the console."

Arguing further would only have gotten me into more trouble, so I kept my mouth shut.

Mom wrapped her arms around me in a hug I didn't return. "I love you, Mac," she said, "and I want you to become everything you were made to be. Video games won't do that for you. All this other stuff you've been doing this summer — well, the good stuff, at least, like building a fort and playing basketball with friends? It will."

After Mom left the room, I realized something. I'm not grounded. I may not be able to play video games anymore, but I can still hang out with Grayson and Justin. I can still go to the fort. I can still go to the pool.

And, since I don't have a gaming console to earn back anymore, I don't have to write another page in this stupid journal.

Dear Mission Diary,

I know I said I didn't have to write in this thing anymore, but the truth is I kind of like doing it. Plus, I was only a couple of pages away from filling the whole stupid book, and it seemed kind of silly to not use up the rest of the pages.

The last couple of days have been pretty amazing, believe it or not. Grayson finally got his electric scooter, and it's awesome. It's got a seat on the back of it, so one of us can stand and drive it while the other one sits on the seat. We rode it over to Justin's house one day and that kid next door to him offered to pay us for a ride. One thing led to another, and now we have a nice little scooter-ride business going. Grayson makes most of the money, of course, since it's his scooter, but I'm helping with scooter-maintenance and helping run the business, so I get a cut, too. I've already paid Mom and Dad back for the carpet cleaning, and now I'm saving up my earnings to buy an electric scooter of my own. Of course, Grayson, Justin, and I also want to go zip-lining, go-carting, and a bunch of other stuff this summer, so it might take a while.

Regardless, even though my mission to get Jerry back failed, I've had some unbelievable fun so far this summer, and summer break's only half over. In fact, I've decided to embark on a new mission: Operation Best Summer Ever.

I'm not just talking about the best summer ever in MY life. I'm talking about the best summer ever, of any kid, period. Lucky for Grayson, Justin, and any other kid we end up hanging out with this summer, they get to come along for the ride.

And it's going to be one heck of a ride!

Look for more of Mac's Missions, coming soon!

If you enjoyed Mac's Mission Diary:
Operation Save the Summer,
please take a moment to visit the
Amazon page and leave a review.

Also … please tell your friends!

Thank you!

Acknowledgements

A book like this takes a lot of effort and teamwork to come together and I've benefitted greatly from the time and talents of many wonderful people.. I'd like to especially thank:

Ken Darby for his immense generosity and patience in completing the interior design.

Afif Amrullah for his beautiful drawings and artwork.

Suzanne, Michelle, Laura, Anton, Susanna, and everyone else who weighed in on the content and cover.

Most especially, I'd like to thank my children for allowing me to air a wee bit of our dirty laundry (lice, ants, and a few quirky character traits) within the pages of Mac's diary. You all provide an immense amount of inspiration and even more joy, blessings, and love.

About the Author

S.J. Engelman lives in Indianapolis, Indiana with a family that looks an awful lot like Mac's—though it now includes two dogs and four chickens in addition to the cat. When not writing, S.J. loves to do anything outdoors, including camping, creek stomping, hiking, and mountain biking. S.J. is a popular speaker on matters of faith and finding joy amidst struggles, and is also the author of the young adult novel *A Single Bead.*

A publication of Inkwell Media, LLC

Made in United States
Orlando, FL
13 May 2025

61247972R00077